The Facts About Flirting

Two of a Kind™

ATTENTION: ORGANIZATIONS AND CORPORATIONS

Most HarperEntertainment books are available at special quantity discounts for bulk purchases for sales promotions, premiums, or fund-raising. For information, please call or write:
**Special Markets Department, HarperCollins Publishers, 10 East 53rd Street, New York, NY 10022-5299
Telephone: (212) 207-7528. Fax: (212) 207-7222.**

The Facts About Flirting

by Judy Katschke

from the series created by
Robert Griffard
& Howard Adler

HarperEntertainment
An Imprint of HarperCollinsPublishers

A PARACHUTE PRESS BOOK

A PARACHUTE PRESS BOOK

Parachute Publishing, L.L.C.
156 Fifth Avenue
Suite 302
New York, NY 10010

Published by
HarperEntertainment
An Imprint of HarperCollins*Publishers*
10 East 53rd Street, New York, NY 10022-5299

TWO OF A KIND books created and produced by Parachute Press, L.L.C., in cooperation with Dualstar Publications, a division of Dualstar Entertainment Group, LLC, published by HarperEntertainment, an imprint of HarperCollins Publishers.

ISBN 0-06-009323-4

HarperCollins®, ® , and HarperEntertainment™ are trademarks of HarperCollins Publishers Inc.

First printing: February 2003

Printed in the United States of America

Visit HarperEntertainment on the World Wide Web at
www.harpercollins.com

10 9 8 7 6 5 4 3 2 1

CHAPTER ONE

"Was that movie at the Student U last night awesome or what?" twelve-year-old Ashley Burke asked. "When the two gymnasts kissed at the end, I couldn't stop crying!"

"You always cry at movies," her sister, Mary-Kate, teased. "That's why your popcorn is always soggy!"

It was Monday morning at the White Oak Academy for Girls. Ashley, Mary-Kate, and their friends sat in the auditorium, waiting for the morning announcements to begin.

Their friend Elise Van Hook turned to face Ashley and Mary-Kate. She smiled, and her glitter-glossed lips sparkled. "I've decided that *Flipping for*

1

You is the most romantic movie ever!" she declared.

Cheryl Miller looked down the row of seats at Ashley. "And speaking of romantic," she said, "I saw you sitting next to Ross at the movie. Did you two have fun?"

Ross Lambert was Ashley's boyfriend and a student at the Harrington School for Boys just down the road. White Oak and Harrington shared classes, sports, and special activities together.

Fun? Ashley thought. *Hardly.* "Ross was laughing throughout the whole movie," Ashley admitted. "He kept calling it a dumb chick flick!"

"Ross was probably just showing off for his friends," Cheryl replied. "A bunch of Harrington guys were sitting in the back row, making gagging noises. I guess they didn't like the movie either."

"Sometimes boys are so disgusting," Ashley said. "Every time Ross ate popcorn last night, he licked his fingers. Then I heard him trying to suck the kernels out of his teeth. And at one point he even burped!"

"Ewwww!" Summer Sorenson cried.

"Why didn't I notice Ross's gross habits before?" Ashley wondered.

Ashley's roommate, Phoebe Cahill, smiled. Her eyes twinkled behind her blue-framed glasses.

"Maybe because you were too busy noticing Ross's big brown eyes?" she asked.

Ashley felt herself blush. *Phoebe is right*, she thought.

"Oh, well," she said. "Who needs guys to tell us what movies to like? *Flipping for You* rocked!"

"No way," Mary-Kate declared. "I agree with Ross. That movie was cornier than cornflakes!"

Ashley shook her head. Sometimes she just didn't get her sister. Sure, they looked alike—both of them had blond hair and blue eyes. But they usually had completely different opinions!

"I noticed that *Jordan* was at the movie, too," Campbell Smith said. She was Mary-Kate's roommate.

"So?" Mary-Kate replied, blushing.

Ashley grinned. Her sister had a *giant* crush on Jordan Marshall, a guy in her fencing class.

"Oh, come on," Phoebe said. "We know you like him."

"No, I don't," Mary-Kate shot back.

"Really?" Summer asked, flipping back her long blond hair. "Is that why at breakfast yesterday you asked me to pass the Jordan instead of the jam?"

Mary-Kate giggled. "Okay, so maybe I do like him a little," she admitted. "But it doesn't matter if

I like him. Jordan thinks of me as a fencing buddy."

"That's because he doesn't know you like him," Ashley said. "I bet he'd ask you out if you tried flirting with him."

Mary-Kate shook her head. "No way. I'm not good at flirting."

"What do you mean, you're not good at flirting?" Ashley replied. "It's easy."

"Not for me," Mary-Kate explained. "Every time I've tried it, either my mouth gets dry, my knees start to shake, or I totally wimp out!"

The other girls nodded their heads in sympathy.

"Maybe if you try to flirt with Jordan it will be easier," Elise said. "After all, he is perfect for you!"

"He's funny," Phoebe added.

"And athletic," Cheryl pointed out.

"And you two get along really well," Ashley finished.

"Okay, okay," Mary-Kate said, holding up her hands. "*Maybe* I'll flirt with him."

"Cool!" Ashley cried. "I can totally help you."

"Whoa," Mary-Kate replied. "I said maybe. I didn't say I'd definitely do it."

Ashley rolled her eyes. *Mary-Kate can be so stubborn sometimes*, she thought. *Can't she tell this is the right thing to do?*

A microphone screeched onstage. Ashley turned and saw Mrs. Pritchard, the headmistress of White Oak, standing at the podium. She was wearing a gray pantsuit and a pink blouse with a white collar.

"Good morning, girls," Mrs. Pritchard said. "I have a very special announcement to make."

Ashley leaned forward in her seat. *What could it be?* she wondered.

"Mr. Burwald, the headmaster at Harrington, has invited us to join in celebrating Harrington's one hundred and fiftieth anniversary," Mrs. Pritchard explained.

"Wow, Harrington was founded a long time ago," Mary-Kate whispered.

"They didn't even have telephones back then!" Phoebe added.

"Wow, thank goodness for E-mail," Summer chimed in.

Ashley rolled her eyes. Summer was always saying ditzy things like that!

"There will be a special Founders Day Ball a week from Friday," Mrs. Pritchard went on.

Excited whispers filled the auditorium.

Mrs. Pritchard held up a hand for silence. "But that's not all," she said. "For a week before the ball, both schools will have Victorian workshops where you can learn what the styles and customs were like one hundred and fifty years ago."

"That sounds fun!" Ashley cried.

"You're all expected to come to the ball in full 1800s dress," Mrs. Pritchard added. "You'll have access to the theater department's costumes. And you'll get to use the skills you learn in the workshops to behave like proper ladies and gentlemen."

"Awesome!" Cheryl cheered. "We're going to party like it's—1899!"

"All of the First Formers have been assigned to different workshop committees that are posted outside the auditorium," Mrs. Pritchard announced. "Look for your name on the way out. You will be teaching your classmates, who are required to attend two workshops each."

The girls stood up to leave.

"I hope I get the Dance Committee," Cheryl said.

"I want the Fashion Committee," Phoebe added.

Me, too, Ashley thought. She loved anything that had to do with clothing!

"Phoebe, we *have* to write about this for the *Acorn*!" Ashley exclaimed. The *Acorn* was the First Form newspaper. She and Phoebe were the editors.

"Definitely," Phoebe agreed. "We can write all

about the ball. You know, who wore what, who danced with whom . . . "

"Maybe we can even make the newspaper a special Founders Day edition!" Ashley suggested. "Let's go talk to Mrs. Pritchard about it right now."

Ashley waved good-bye to her friends as she and Phoebe made their way to the front of the room.

"Hello, girls," Mrs. Pritchard said as they approached the stage. "I'm glad you're here."

"Mrs. Pritchard, we have a great idea for Founders Day," Ashley said.

"So do I," Mrs. Pritchard said. "I'd like you to do a special article on the festivities."

Ashley looked at Phoebe. Excellent! Mrs. Pritchard was already on board!

"We have lots of ideas—" Phoebe began.

"Actually, I already have an idea for you," Mrs. Pritchard cut in. "Mr. Burwald asked that you write a feature article on Phineas T. Harrington III."

Ashley wrinkled her nose. "Who's that?" she asked.

"Phineas was the founder of the Harrington School," Mrs. Pritchard explained. "From what I hear, he was one heck of a guy!"

"Really?" Phoebe asked excitedly. "What was so interesting about him?"

"Plenty!" Mrs. Pritchard replied. "Phineas collected stamps, played the harpsichord, and had the longest beard in all of New Hampshire."

Ashley and Phoebe raised their eyebrows at each other.

Great, Ashley thought. *With all the fun stuff going on for Founders Day, we get stuck with the most boring assignment in history!*

CHAPTER TWO

As Mary-Kate left the main building, she wrapped a thick gray scarf around her neck. She was usually psyched about her fencing class. But that morning she was faced with her sister's challenge: to flirt . . . or not to flirt?

"Mary-Kate, wait up!" Campbell called. "I'm going to the gym, too."

Mary-Kate shivered in the February cold as she waited for her roommate to catch up. Campbell was dressed in a bulky stadium jacket and a baseball cap.

"Hi, Campbell," Mary-Kate said. "Did you find out what committee you're on?"

"The Cooking Committee." Campbell groaned.

"I hope they ate tuna sandwiches in the 1800s, because that's all I know how to make."

Mary-Kate giggled. Campbell was a terrific athlete. But a not-so-terrific cook!

"What committee are you on?" Campbell asked.

Mary-Kate's smile turned into a frown. "I couldn't find my name on any list," she replied. "I guess I'll ask Mrs. Pritchard about it later."

Campbell tilted her head as she studied Mary-Kate. "Is that the reason for the gloom-and-doom face?" she asked. "Because you weren't picked for a committee?"

"Not really," Mary-Kate admitted.

"Then, what?" Campbell pressed.

"It's Jordan," Mary-Kate admitted. "Do you think I should flirt with him?"

"No way." Campbell shook her head. "Flirting is dumb! My way of getting a date is much more effective."

"What is it?" Mary-Kate asked.

"Just look Jordan straight in the eye and say, 'Movies. Saturday. Eight o'clock. Be there,'" Campbell explained.

"Wow," Mary-Kate said. "That is so . . . direct!" *I could never be that bold*, she thought.

"Hey, life is like baseball," Campbell replied. "Do

you want to play the game? Or sit in the dugout?"

"I want to play the game," Mary-Kate said as they entered the Sports Complex. "But what if Jordan says no?"

"He won't," Campbell said. "Now, get your game face on and go for it!"

"Okay, thanks," Mary-Kate replied.

The two girls rapped knuckles. Campbell left for basketball practice on the second floor. Mary-Kate headed into the main-floor locker room.

Can I really do this? Mary-Kate wondered as she opened her locker. But as she changed into her fencing bodysuit, she began to feel more daring.

I can do this! she thought. *I don't have to flirt. I just have to be real.*

She left the locker room and entered the gym. Mary-Kate grabbed a mesh face mask and plopped it on her head.

I will ask Jordan out, Mary-Kate decided. *In fact, I'll ask him out as soon as I see him!*

"Mary-Kate," a voice called. "Over here!"

Mary-Kate turned. Jordan was sitting on the bleachers, waving at her. Instantly, her legs turned to Jell-O. "H-hi, Jordan!" she stammered.

On the other hand, Mary-Kate thought, *maybe I'll wait until my knees stop shaking.*

11

"I saved you a space," Jordan said, patting the seat next to him.

Mary-Kate smiled and sat down. Jordan always looked cute in his fencing gear. He always looked cute, period! "Why is everyone sitting on the bleachers?" she asked.

Jordan ran a hand through his sandy-blond hair. "Coach Slotsky is going to make a special announcement," he said. "Something about Founders Day."

Coach Slotsky entered the gym. He had a long mustache that curled at the ends, and he liked to use a lot of French words—even though he wasn't French!

"*Bonjour!*" Coach Slotsky greeted the class. "I want to announce that fencing will be a major part of the upcoming Victorian demonstrations."

"What's so 1800s about fencing?" Mary-Kate asked.

"Good question, Mademoiselle Burke!" Coach Slotsky exclaimed. "Fencing was a very popular sport in the 1800s. It was used to show skill and sometimes to settle an argument."

Coach Slotsky went on to explain that the class would perform a special fencing demonstration before the ball. Everyone in class would be involved.

That's why I wasn't picked for a committee, Mary-Kate realized. *I'll be too busy showing off my fencing skills!*

Then she had another thought.

"Do you think Coach Slotsky will make us partners, Jordan?" Mary-Kate whispered. *That would be perfect,* she thought. *Then we'd be hanging out a lot!*

"Sure!" Jordan said. "Coach Slotsky always teams us up to practice."

Mary-Kate's shoulders slumped. *Team* was a major buddy word. *Not* a date word.

"We'll talk more about the demonstration at the end of class," Coach Slotsky said. "In the meantime, let's do some warm-up lunges."

Mary-Kate's heart pounded as she watched Jordan climb off the bleachers. She got up and followed him.

Don't sit in the dugout, Mary-Kate reminded herself. *Play the game.*

"Um, Jordan?" she called.

"Yeah?" Jordan replied, turning. His green eyes flashed at her.

Mary-Kate opened her mouth to speak, but nothing came out.

"What's up?" Jordan asked.

13

Just say it already! Mary-Kate told herself. She took a deep breath. "Jordan, will you—"

WHACK!

Mary-Kate's fencing mask dropped over her face. She stood frozen as she stared at Jordan through a sea of mesh.

Jordan burst out laughing. "Nice move!" he said.

How embarrassing! Mary-Kate thought, yanking off the mask.

"You should have seen your face just now!" Jordan said, still laughing. "So, what did you want to ask me, Mary-Kate?"

Mary-Kate felt her cheeks burn. No way could she ask him out now! "Forget it," she said. "It was nothing important."

CHAPTER THREE

"Who cares that Phineas T. Harrington III liked fresh eggs so much that he had his own henhouse?" Ashley moaned. "That is so totally boring!"

It was Monday afternoon. Ashley and Phoebe were in the school library, flipping through encyclopedias and looking up information for their article.

"The dresses girls wore back then weren't boring," Phoebe said. She pointed to a picture of two women wearing floor-length dresses that flared out in a large hoop shape at the bottom. "They were extreme!"

Ashley wasn't surprised that Phoebe liked the dresses. Her roommate loved vintage clothes!

"How did women fit through doorways back

then?" Ashley wondered. "Didn't the hoopskirt get in the way?"

"Maybe doorways were wider in those days," Phoebe guessed.

Ashley sighed. *There has to be* something *exciting about Phineas T. Harrington III!* she thought. She opened another book and stared at a portrait on the first page. It was a picture of a dark-haired woman with big, sad eyes.

"Who's that?" Phoebe peered over Ashley's shoulder.

"Her name was Lucretia Arsdale," Ashley read. "She used to live on the White Oak Academy grounds before the school was built."

"She was so fashionable," Phoebe read on. "Her skirts were wider than any of the other ladies' skirts in New Hampshire."

"Lucretia sounds cool," Ashley said. "Too bad we can't write an article about her."

"Maybe we can!" Phoebe cried. "Look!" She jabbed a finger at a paragraph farther down the page.

"Phineas T. Harrington III was deeply in love with Lucretia Arsdale," Phoebe said. "But Lucretia was already engaged to a wealthy gentleman named Mortimer Baird."

"Bummer," Ashley replied.

"Lucretia's heart really belonged to Phineas," Phoebe continued. "They spent their days sending each other love letters."

"It says that Phineas left his letters inside the trunk of a big white oak tree on Lucretia's estate so Mortimer wouldn't discover them," Ashley said.

"A tree of love! Cool!" Phoebe gasped. "Do you think it still exists?"

Ashley shook her head. "Probably not," she replied. "That was so long ago. I bet the tree was chopped down when White Oak was built."

Phoebe shrugged. "I guess. But wouldn't it be awesome if it were still here?"

"Hey, listen to this!" Ashley said. "'When Mortimer found out about the letters, he challenged Phineas to a fencing duel. But the duel never happened. Lucretia died of pneumonia. Although many swore it was from a broken heart.'"

Ashley sank back in her chair. That was the most romantic story she had ever heard!

"Phoebe!" Ashley cried. "That can be the topic of our article for the *Acorn*. Phineas T. Harrington—incurable romantic."

"Absolutely," Phoebe agreed. "What girl wouldn't want to read about this awesome Victorian Romeo?"

"Phineas seemed like the perfect gentleman,"

Ashley said. *Unlike a certain boyfriend of mine,* she silently added.

"I'll bet Phineas never licked his fingers when he ate popcorn," Ashley went on. "Too bad Ross isn't more like Phineas T. Harrington III."

Ashley and Phoebe decided to check out the book from the library. Then they put on their jackets and headed for their next classes.

"I can't wait to write about Phineas and Lucretia's love affair," Phoebe said. "Our article is going to rock."

Ashley nodded in agreement. "See you later," she said, hugging the book to her chest.

The two girls left the library. Phoebe headed for the English Building, Ashley toward the Math Complex.

Ashley heard birds chirping in a nearby tree. *That's weird,* she thought. She hadn't heard birds chirping all winter.

Ashley looked up at the branches to see what kind of birds were singing. Her eyes fell on something carved into the tree trunk.

Her eyes widened as she stared at the trunk. *No way,* she thought. *It can't be.*

But it was. Carved high up on the tree was PH ❤ LA. Phineas Harrington loves Lucretia Arsdale!

Ashley jumped up and down. "I found it!" she cried. "I found the tree of love!"

The next morning Ashley dragged Phoebe across campus to show her the tree.

"You're right!" Phoebe exclaimed. "This is actually the tree of love. And look!" She pointed to the tree trunk. "That hole is perfect for holding love letters."

"I'm already two steps ahead of you," Ashley said. "Let's give this baby a test run!"

"You mean put love letters in the tree?" Phoebe cried. "But you already have a boyfriend."

"I wasn't thinking about *me*," Ashley said. "We need to find someone who is madly in love with a guy but too shy to tell him."

"Like who?" Phoebe asked.

"Duh!" Ashley exclaimed. "Mary-Kate is too shy to flirt with Jordan. The tree is the perfect way to bring them together!"

"Oh, yeah!" Phoebe said. "So what should we do?"

The two girls thought for a second.

"Well," Ashley said, "I can write an unsigned love letter to Jordan and ask him to leave his answer in the tree."

Phoebe's dark curls bounced as she nodded. "I

19

get it!" she replied. "And when Jordan responds—you can slip that letter to Mary-Kate!"

Ashley's heart beat faster as she thought through her plan. "Then Mary-Kate will write the next letter, and so on and so on," she declared. "Until Mary-Kate and Jordan are so in love that they have to meet!"

Ashley and Phoebe high-fived.

"Brilliant!" Phoebe cried. "We'll be bringing Mary-Kate together with the boy of her dreams and she won't even know it!"

And the sooner the better, Ashley thought. She reached into her backpack and whipped out a notebook and pen.

"Now, remember," Ashley said. "You can't tell Mary-Kate about the love letters. We don't want to make her nervous."

"Got it," Phoebe agreed.

Ashley pressed her pen against the notebook and began to write. "My true love . . . my heart dances with joy when you speak. My eyes sparkle when I see you. Write back and put your letter inside the big oak tree next to the library. My heart will flutter when I read it."

"Ashley, you're a modern-day cupid!" Phoebe said.

"Thanks," Ashley said. She ripped out the page and folded it. "I have the perfect finishing touch."

"What is it?" Phoebe asked.

"A splash of Dazzling Daisy," Ashley replied. She pulled a tiny bottle of perfume from her jacket pocket and gently sprayed the letter.

"Good idea," Phoebe said. She glanced over Ashley's shoulder. "Ohmigosh. There's Jordan!"

Ashley spun around. Jordan was heading toward the library. "Let's follow him," she said. "We can stash the letter in his backpack when he's not looking."

"This is too wild!" Phoebe exclaimed. "Do you think it's going to work?"

"Hey, it worked for Phineas and Lucretia," Ashley replied with a grin. "Come on, Phoebe. All systems go!"

CHAPTER FOUR

"I never should have used the direct approach," Mary-Kate told Ashley. She flopped onto her bed. It was midday break on Tuesday, and she had just told Ashley about her embarrassing moment with Jordan.

"Don't worry," Ashley said. "There's still hope for you and Jordan."

I doubt it, Mary-Kate thought. "I made a fool of myself," she replied. "I can't tell him I like him now."

Ashley smiled and sat on the bed next to Mary-Kate. "Well, then there's only one thing left to do," she declared. "Flirt!"

"I was afraid you'd say that." Mary-Kate sighed.

"Mary-Kate!" Ashley cried. "If you don't let

Jordan know you like him, some other girl might beat you to it."

Mary-Kate sat up. Jordan with another girl? She couldn't let that happen. Even if it meant doing something she never thought she would ever do!

I guess I have to give it a try, Mary-Kate thought. "Okay," she agreed. "But where do I start?"

"It's simple," Ashley said, jumping off the bed. "You just have to know the facts about flirting."

"The facts about flirting?" Mary-Kate repeated.

Ashley nodded. "The next time you speak to Jordan, look him straight in the eye and don't lose eye contact!"

"You mean stare at him?" Mary-Kate asked. "I don't know, Ashley. I wouldn't want Jordan staring at me! It would make me feel embarrassed."

"Trust me," Ashley replied. "When I first started dating Ross, we would stare into each other's eyes for hours."

"Really?" Mary-Kate asked.

"Well, maybe not hours," Ashley said. "More like seconds. But it was soooo romantic!"

Mary-Kate shrugged. "If you say so."

"And boys *love* compliments," Ashley went on. "So be sure to flatter Jordan as much as possible."

"That's easy. I can tell him what a great athlete he

is!" Mary-Kate decided. "What should I do next?"

"Boys love hearing girls say their names," Ashley said. "So try to say his name a lot."

"Jordan, Jordan, Jordan," Mary-Kate practiced. *That wasn't so hard*, she thought. *I kind of like saying Jordan's name!* "What's next?"

Ashley shrugged. "That's it!"

"That's it?" Mary-Kate repeated. She couldn't believe how easy flirting was. *Why did I think this was so hard?* she wondered.

"Yup," Ashley said. "So are you going to flirt with Jordan in your next fencing class?"

"You bet," Mary-Kate replied. She couldn't wait to try it out!

"Jordan, Jordan, Jordan," Mary-Kate whispered to herself. She was rushing across campus to her fencing class. Mists of cold air formed in front of her mouth as she repeated his name. But inside she felt all warm and fuzzy—the way she always felt when she was around Jordan!

Mary-Kate reached the Sports Complex and hurried inside. Her eyes scanned the gym. Students were already warming up by doing lunges.

Where is he? Mary-Kate wondered. She spotted Jordan across the gym, adjusting his fencing mask.

Here goes nothing, Mary-Kate thought as she tried to calm the butterflies in her stomach. "Hi, Jordan!" she called.

Jordan smiled. "Hey, Mary-Kate!" he said.

So far so good, Mary-Kate thought. She walked up to Jordan and stared him straight in the eye.

"What's up, Jordan?" Mary-Kate asked. She tried not to blink as she looked at him.

"Same old . . . stuff," Jordan said slowly, staring back.

Compliment him, Mary-Kate reminded herself. "Did you know you're the best fencer in the whole class . . . Jordan?" she asked.

Mary-Kate watched Jordan turn a deep shade of red. "Th-thanks," he stammered.

"Could you show me one of your awesome lunges, Jordan?" Mary-Kate went on.

"Um, okay," Jordan mumbled. He picked up his sword and practiced a lunge. But he lunged too far forward and fell flat on his face!

"Ohmigosh—Jordan!" Mary-Kate exclaimed. She helped him up. "Are you okay?"

"F-fine," Jordan stammered. "Excuse me."

Mary-Kate watched Jordan hurry out of the gym. *That wasn't how it was supposed to go at all,* she thought. *What did I do wrong?*

CHAPTER FIVE

"Do you want to look inside the tree of love, or should I?" Ashley asked Phoebe.

It was two days after Ashley had slipped Jordan the secret love letter. So far there had been no response.

"You do it," Phoebe said. "But hurry, we can't be late for class."

Ashley reached inside the hole and felt a thin, flat piece of paper.

"A letter!" Ashley shrieked. "Jordan wrote back!"

"Read it, read it!" Phoebe said excitedly.

Ashley unfolded the plain white paper. The letter was typed on a computer. "'My love . . . getting your letter made me happier than watching a sunset on a sandy white beach . . . '" she read.

"How poetic!" Phoebe said.

"'Your letter was sweeter than wildflowers in spring,'" Ashley went on.

"How passionate!" Phoebe gasped.

Ashley stared at the letter. "Mary-Kate really lucked out," she said. "I've never read anything so incredibly romantic in my whole life."

"Who knew that Jordan Marshall would turn out to be a modern-day Lord Byron?" Phoebe asked.

"Lord who?" Ashley asked.

"Lord Byron was a romantic writer in the 1800s," Phoebe explained. "But Jordan has him beat!"

Ashley's and Phoebe's gloves thumped as they exchanged high fives.

Phoebe studied the paper in Ashley's hand. "But why didn't Jordan sign his letter?"

"Jordan probably thinks Mary-Kate will *know* it's from him," Ashley replied. She folded the letter and carefully placed it inside her backpack. "Now all we have to do is sneak the letter to Mary-Kate."

"When are you going to do that?" Phoebe asked.

"During our biology class tomorrow," Ashley said. "It'll be easier with lots of kids around."

"Class!" Phoebe cried. "We're going to be late."

"Yikes!" Ashley exclaimed. "We'd better move it."

Ashley and Phoebe raced across campus.

"When this all comes together," Phoebe said, "Mary-Kate will be so lucky to have a boyfriend like Jordan."

"That's for sure," Ashley agreed. Then she thought about her own boyfriend.

"Ross would never send me a letter like that," she went on. "I think he totally forgot how to be romantic."

"So remind him," Phoebe suggested. "Make him do some romantic stuff with you."

That sounds like a good plan, Ashley thought. Maybe there was hope for a romantic Ross after all.

"Hey, Ross," Ashley said that evening. "What do you feel like doing tonight?"

Ashley and Ross were together for a special First Former Game Night. But Ashley's mind wasn't on Ping-Pong or video games. It was Operation Romantic Ross!

"As soon as the Morons from Mars game is free, let's go for it," Ross answered. "We still hold the team record for most morons mutilated!"

Ashley frowned. She and Ross were sitting on beanbag chairs and eating popcorn. Ross was licking his fingers—as usual!

"Before we play Morons from Mars, can we do something else?" Ashley asked.

"Sure, what do you want to do?" Ross replied. "Try out Celestial Patrol Squad? I heard that game rocks!"

"I don't want to play a game." Ashley leaned over her beanbag chair and smiled. "Why don't you whisper something in my ear? You know, something soft . . . and sweet." *And romantic*, she thought.

"Soft and sweet?" Ross repeated.

"Mmm-hmm." Ashley nodded.

"Okay," Ross said. He put his popcorn box on the floor and leaned closer to Ashley.

Ashley smiled and closed her eyes. Phoebe was right. Ross could be romantic. All she had to do was remind him!

Ross put his lips near Ashley's ear. "Marshmallow."

Ashley's eyes popped open. "Huh?"

Ross laughed. "You said you wanted me to whisper something soft and sweet, right?" he asked. "Come on. That was funny!"

Ashley began to smile. But then she stopped. *So what if it was funny*, she thought. *Can't Ross be romantic for five seconds?*

"Hey, let's go!" Ross pointed to the row of video games. "Morons from Mars is free."

29

Oh, well, Ashley thought as she watched Ross run over to the game. She was about to join him, when she spotted Jordan. He was kneeling by the CD player.

I bet Jordan would have whispered something soft and sweet in Mary-Kate's ear, Ashley thought. *And it would not have been "marshmallow"!*

CHAPTER SIX

"Wow!" Ashley gasped in biology class. "Check this out, Mary-Kate."

Mary-Kate looked up from her microscope. She saw Ashley staring into her eyepiece with an excited smile.

"What do you see?" Mary-Kate asked.

"Tons of pink specks," Ashley replied. "I wonder what it is."

Mary-Kate peered through the eyepiece on Ashley's microscope. She immediately recognized the glittery pink stuff.

"So what do you think?" Ashley asked. "What is it? Did I just make a meaningful scientific discovery or something?"

"Yeah," Mary-Kate answered. "You discovered the effects of lip gloss on a slide!"

"Lip gloss!" Ashley rubbed her palm over the slide. "Whoops."

Mary-Kate returned to her own microscope. Usually she loved biology. But today she felt totally bummed out.

"What do *you* see on your slide, Mary-Kate?" Ashley asked.

"Oh, nothing interesting." Mary-Kate sighed. "Just like my life."

"Come on," Ashley said. "Your flirting couldn't have been that bad!"

Mary-Kate pictured her last meeting with Jordan. "Trust me," she replied. "It was."

"Did you do what we talked about?" Ashley asked.

Mary-Kate nodded. "I did everything you told me to do."

"And?" Ashley prompted.

"And he ran away!" Mary-Kate cried.

Ashley looked stunned. "You're kidding," she said.

"Nope." Mary-Kate shook her head. "See, this proves it. I'm not good at flirting."

"Maybe you just need some practice," Ashley

suggested. "Why don't you try again? I bet it will work next time."

The last thing I want to do is try flirting again, Mary-Kate thought. But she really wanted to go out with Jordan. "I'll think about it," she replied.

"Okay, class!" Mr. Barber, the biology teacher, called out. "Now that you've studied your slides, begin writing down your findings."

Mary-Kate grabbed her blue spiral notebook and opened it to a fresh page. Just as she was about to write, she noticed a piece of paper sticking out between the pages.

What's this? Mary-Kate wondered.

She unfolded the paper. " . . . Beach at sunset . . . sweeter than wildflowers?"

A love letter? Mary-Kate thought. *In* my *notebook?* "I don't believe it!" she cried.

Everyone looked up from their microscopes.

"Did you find something interesting, Mary-Kate?" Mr. Barber asked.

"No, Mr. Barber," Mary-Kate blurted out, shoving the letter under the counter. "Just the same old . . . germs."

"Remember, Mary-Kate," Mr. Barber pointed out, "germs play an important role in the world of science."

Mary-Kate nodded. But as soon as Mr. Barber looked away, she turned back to the letter.

"Ashley!" Mary-Kate whispered. She tugged at her sister's charcoal-colored sweater. "You've got to read this!"

Ashley smiled as she read the letter to herself. "Whoa," she said. "Looks like you have a secret admirer."

"No kidding," Mary-Kate replied. She glanced over her shoulder at the boys in class. "But who do you think sent it?"

Ashley shrugged. "I have no idea."

Mary-Kate's heart pounded as she read the letter again. "This is too weird," she said. "Whoever it is wants me to leave my reply in some oak tree on campus."

"Excellent!" Ashley replied. "How romantic."

"I've heard of E-mail," Mary-Kate said, "but I've never heard of tree mail!"

"Are you going to write back?" Ashley asked.

Mary-Kate studied the letter again. *Is this letter really for me?* she wondered. "I don't know," she admitted. "What do you think I should do?"

"You *have* to write back!" Ashley insisted. "How many girls here can say that they have a real secret admirer?"

Ashley's right, Mary-Kate thought. She had never gotten a secret love letter before. Come to think of it—she had never gotten *any* love letter before!

"Okay," Mary-Kate decided. "I'll do it."

"Great!" Ashley exclaimed. "Just make sure you say something romantic."

"Romantic?" Mary-Kate cried. "I don't even know how to flirt. How am I supposed to write a romantic letter?"

"Not a problem," Ashley said. "I'll help you."

"Thanks, Ashley," Mary-Kate said. "You're the best!"

"Write this down, Mary-Kate," Ashley said that night in the Student U. She cleared her throat. "Your letter made my heart dance with happiness—"

Is she kidding? Mary-Kate thought. "Too corny!" she cut in.

"Okay, then try this," Ashley suggested. "Your letter was more precious than the rarest gem—"

I don't think so. Mary-Kate rolled her eyes. "Too sappy," she interrupted.

Ashley turned in her beanbag chair to face Mary-Kate. "Excuse me!" she protested. "I thought you wanted your letter to sound romantic."

"I do," Mary-Kate said. "But I also want it to

sound like me. Maybe I should write it myself."

Ashley looked disappointed. "Fine," she said. "But can I see it when you're finished?"

Mary-Kate paused. On one hand, she wanted Ashley to read it. But on the other hand, if she did, Ashley would probably make her rewrite the whole thing!

"This should be between me and my secret admirer," Mary-Kate said.

"Okay, I guess you're right." Ashley shrugged. She stood up to leave. "But can you at least *try* to sound romantic?"

"I'll try," Mary-Kate promised.

Her sister gave a little wave and left the Student U.

Mary-Kate thought for a second. Then she began to write. *Dear Secret Admirer . . . Your letter was as sweet as a powdered sugar doughnut with jelly!*

Mary-Kate looked at the page and wrinkled her nose. *That's lame,* she thought. She tried again.

Dear Secret Admirer, Your letter was the best thing that happened to me since . . . I hit a homerun on my softball team!

Better, Mary-Kate decided. *But Ashley's right. I should at least be a little romantic. Maybe I'll write a poem.*

Roses are red, Mary-Kate wrote. *Violets are blue.*

Her eyes darted around the U for inspiration. Mary-Kate sucked in her breath. Jordan was at the hot cocoa machine only a few feet away!

He looked adorable in a bulky gray sweater, dark blue jeans, and what looked like brand-new sneakers. Mary-Kate couldn't take her eyes off him.

That's it, Mary-Kate thought. *I have to give flirting another chance!*

Mary-Kate felt her knees wobble as she stood up and walked over to the hot cocoa machine. But she didn't let it stop her.

"Hi, Jordan," she called.

Jordan looked up. "Hi, Mary-Kate," he said.

"How are you?" Mary-Kate asked. "You didn't get hurt from your fall the other day, did you?"

Jordan's cheeks flushed pink. "No, I'm fine," he mumbled as he poured himself some cocoa.

What do I say now? Mary-Kate wondered. "Sooo . . . it's a good day for cocoa," she blurted out.

That was so dumb! she scolded herself.

But Jordan didn't seem to notice. "Yeah," he replied. "It's so cold outside I was starting to grow fur."

Mary-Kate giggled. "Really?" she said. "It's so cold outside my teeth were beginning to curl."

"Oh, yeah?" Jordan shot back. "It's so cold outside my eyeballs are turning into snowballs."

"Gross!" Mary-Kate laughed. She was having so much fun that her knees had stopped shaking.

"Want a cup?" Jordan asked as he put his own cocoa down on the counter.

"Sure," Mary-Kate said. She watched Jordan place another cup under the spout. So far things were going great. Now was the perfect time to start flirting again.

"Wow, Jordan," Mary-Kate said. She pointed to his feet. "Those are awesome sneakers!"

"Thanks," Jordan said as he pressed a green button on the machine. "I just got them at the mall."

So far so good! Mary-Kate thought excitedly. The compliment worked.

"I'll bet you're the best dressed guy at Harrington," Mary-Kate went on. "At least . . . I think so."

Jordan froze. His face turned tomato red.

Uh-oh, Mary-Kate thought. *That's the same look Jordan had on his face before he ran out of the gym!*

"You d-do?" Jordan stammered. "I . . . um . . . yikes!"

Jordan yelped and jumped back. Hot cocoa was oozing over the cup and onto his brand-new sneakers!

Mary-Kate wanted to melt right into the floor. Was she ever going to get this flirting thing right?

"I have to go clean my sneakers," Jordan said quickly. "See you later, Mary-Kate."

Mary-Kate's heart sank as she watched Jordan walk away. *I'd better write something good to my secret admirer,* she decided. *Because I definitely don't stand a chance with Jordan!*

CHAPTER SEVEN

"'Phineas was so secretive about his love for Lucretia that he hid a lock of her hair inside an old pocket watch,'" Phoebe read out loud. She looked up from her notepad. "How does that sound to you, Ashley?"

"Pretty good," Ashley replied.

"All we need is a paragraph about Mortimer Baird," Phoebe suggested. "And we're finished with our article!"

Ashley and Phoebe were walking across campus to their first class. They had spent most of the weekend writing their article about Phineas T. Harrington III. But that morning Ashley's mind wasn't on the newspaper. It was on Mary-Kate!

"Phoebe, I am so psyched that Mary-Kate finally wrote back to Jordan!" Ashley exclaimed.

"Are you sure she wrote back?" Phoebe asked. She slipped the notepad into her backpack.

"That's what Mary-Kate told me at breakfast this morning," Ashley replied. "She said she spent the whole weekend trying to come up with the perfect letter."

"The perfect letter," Phoebe repeated. "Can you imagine how romantic it must be?"

"For sure," Ashley said as they headed down a path near the library. "I wish I could read it."

"So do I," Phoebe agreed. "But we can't."

"Right," Ashley said. *Or can we?* she thought.

Ashley and Phoebe glanced at each other as they walked past the tree of love. Then they started to slow down.

"Phoebe," Ashley said slowly, "maybe we should just look to see if the letter is there. I mean, what if a squirrel carried it off?"

"Or a bird?" Phoebe added. "We'd better check. It's our job to look out for Mary-Kate."

"Right," Ashley said again. Without another word, she and Phoebe raced over to the tree.

"I can see the letter!" Ashley cried as they got closer. "It's in a bright blue envelope."

"But we're not going to read it . . . are we?" Phoebe asked.

"Of course not," Ashley replied, even though inside she was dying to. "This is between Mary-Kate and Jordan."

"Yeah," Phoebe agreed.

The two girls stood there in silence. Ashley folded her arms and stared at the envelope in the tree. Phoebe tapped her foot and sighed.

I can't stand it anymore! Ashley thought. "I *have* to read it, okay!" she cried. Her hand shot inside the tree.

"Go for it!" Phoebe exclaimed.

Ashley ripped open the blue envelope. She unfolded the letter and read: "'Roses are red . . . violets are blue . . . I'm sick of oatmeal . . . how about you?'"

I can't believe it, Ashley thought. *This poem stinks! And it is not romantic!*

"You're kidding," Phoebe said. "That's not what it really says, is it?"

"Yes!" Ashley wailed. "How does Mary-Kate expect to get a date with Jordan with a letter like this?"

"Does the letter at least smell like perfume?" Phoebe asked hopefully.

Ashley wrinkled her nose as she sniffed the letter. "I think it smells like sports rub," she replied.

"Oh, boy. This is seriously bad," Phoebe said.

Ashley paced back and forth in front of the tree. "Mary-Kate cannot send this letter to Jordan," she said.

"Mary-Kate doesn't even *know* it's Jordan," Phoebe pointed out. "So maybe if we *tell* her it's Jordan, she'll write a better letter!"

"No!" Ashley cried. "If Mary-Kate knew her secret admirer was Jordan, she'd be way too nervous to write again!"

"Then why don't we just put Mary-Kate's letter back in the tree and see what happens?" Phoebe asked.

"I don't think so," Ashley replied. *I know Mary-Kate said this should be between her and her secret admirer,* she thought, *but she needs me on this one!* Ashley reached into her backpack and took out a pen and paper.

"What are you doing?" Phoebe asked.

"Helping my sister." Ashley began to write. "Finding your letter was like finding gold at the end of a rainbow . . . a pearl inside an oyster!"

"But, Ashley . . . " Phoebe said. "Are you sure you're doing the right thing?"

Ashley smiled as she searched for her perfume

bottle. Of course she was. She was doing it in the name of *love*!

"Trust me," Ashley said, spraying the letter. "When Mary-Kate finds out what I did for her, she's going to thank me!"

CHAPTER EIGHT

"Be careful, you guys," Mary-Kate warned her friends. "The last time we ate pizza in my room, I found a pepperoni inside my sneaker two days later."

It was Tuesday night at Porter House. Seven friends sat cross-legged on the floor of Mary-Kate and Campbell's room around two jumbo-size pizza boxes.

It had been almost a week since Mary-Kate found her secret admirer's first romantic letter inside her backpack. Since then they had been sending letters back and forth through the big oak tree.

So far only Ashley and Campbell knew about the secret letters. And that's how Mary-Kate wanted to keep it. To be honest, she wasn't that excited about them anymore. Whoever this guy was, he seemed way too corny for her!

"Hey, Elise," Cheryl asked. "Since when do you eat pizza with a knife and fork?"

Elise daintily cut her pizza slice. "A real Victorian lady would never eat pizza with her hands," she said. "That's what I learned from my Victorian Manners Committee."

"They probably didn't have pizza in those days," Ashley said, popping a cheesy mushroom into her mouth.

"It's a good thing," Summer pointed out. "Just one slice would bust a lady's corset wide open!"

"What's a corset?" Campbell asked.

"It's what girls laced around their bodies to make their waists seem smaller," Summer explained. "I learned all about it on the Fashion Committee."

"Oh, great!" Campbell said. "Do we have to wear corsets to the ball?"

"No," Summer replied, shaking her head. "Those Victorian dresses are tight enough."

"How is your Dance Committee coming along, Cheryl?" Mary-Kate asked. "Is everyone getting funky Victorian style?"

"As if!" Cheryl laughed. "Dances in those days

were all about curtsies and bows and sweeping hand in hand across a ballroom floor."

"That sounds romantic," Phoebe said.

"I know," Cheryl agreed. "Dancing couples had to hold at least one hand. And the man usually placed the other hand on the woman's waist."

"What if he had sweaty hands?" Elise asked.

"In that case, he placed a handkerchief under his sweaty palm," Cheryl explained, "to protect his partner's dress."

"A handkerchief!" Phoebe exclaimed. "How gentlemanly."

"Not if he already used it to blow his nose," Campbell joked.

Everyone laughed as they chowed down.

"Here's another thing I learned about the 1800s," Cheryl went on. "Victorian girls had to dance with every guy who asked them."

"At the same time?" Summer gasped.

"No, Summer," Cheryl said. "Each guy had to sign a dance card and wait his turn."

"Do you think we'll have dance cards at the Founders Day Ball?" Ashley asked.

"That's what I heard," Cheryl replied.

Mary-Kate tried to imagine a Victorian dance card. *It's not such a bad idea*, she thought. *Maybe it will get my secret admirer to finally sign his name!*

"I know!" Elise exclaimed. "Let's make lists of all the boys we want to dance with at the ball."

"And after the ball we can compare our lists with our dance cards," Summer suggested, "to see how many guys we liked asked us to dance."

"I'll get some stuff to write on," Cheryl offered. She turned to Mary-Kate. "Do you keep paper in your desk?"

Mary-Kate nodded. "Top drawer. Right-hand side."

Cheryl opened the drawer. "Here's some," she said, holding up a bunch of paper. "Hey, what's this?"

Mary-Kate froze. Her letters! "Um, nothing!" she cried.

"Whoa," Cheryl said, shuffling through the papers. "These are love letters!"

"Love letters?" everyone shrieked.

"I didn't know you had a boyfriend, Mary-Kate," Summer said. "Is it your fencing hottie?"

Mary-Kate thought about her last encounter with Jordan. "Definitely not," she replied.

"Then tell us who he is!" Elise begged.

"I wish I knew," Mary-Kate admitted. She took a deep breath and filled her friends in on the story.

"A secret admirer!" Elise cried. "Cool."

"Hey, listen to this," Cheryl said as she read out loud. "'How do I love thee? Let me count the ways . . . Your words linger in my thoughts and dreams . . . .'"

Mary-Kate blushed. "I don't know why he keeps writing stuff like that," she said. "My letters are nowhere near as corny."

"Well, I think this mystery guy is awesome," Ashley chimed in.

"Definitely," Phoebe agreed. "He should be writing sonnets."

"Or at least writing for Hallmark," Summer added.

"Actually, I think he's kind of boring," Mary-Kate admitted.

"Are you crazy?" Ashley cried. "No way is this guy boring. Maybe you're just getting bored with all the letter-writing."

"Yeah," Phoebe added. "It might be time to take it to the next level."

Mary-Kate raised her eyebrows. "What's the next level?"

"You have to meet him face-to-face!" Phoebe exclaimed.

"Meet him?" Mary-Kate asked. "How?"

"By getting a date with him," Ashley suggested. "It's the only way you'll find out who this mystery guy is."

"Come on, Mary-Kate," Cheryl said. "Go for it!"

Mary-Kate shrugged. *Do I really want to do this?* she wondered. All her friends seemed to think it was a good idea. "Sure," she said. "I'll meet him."

Everyone cheered.

"But remember!" Elise said. "A proper Victorian lady would never ask a gentleman out on a date. She would wait until he asked her."

"Bor-ring!" Campbell sang.

"Don't worry," Elise told Mary-Kate. "Just write in your letters that you're *dying* to meet him. I bet he will ask you to the ball."

Mary-Kate turned to Ashley. "Maybe we can double at the ball," she said. "Me and my Romeo and you and your Romeo."

"I *wish* Ross were my Romeo." Ashley sighed.

Mary-Kate grabbed another slice of pizza. *Oh, well,* she thought. *I'm going to have to meet this guy sooner or later.*

After all, he can't be a secret forever!

CHAPTER NINE

"So, Ashley," Phoebe asked. "Do you have everything you need?"

Ashley nodded. "My faux-fur jacket for a stroll in the moonlight . . . your antique lace handkerchief . . . a dab of perfume . . . "

I hope this works, Ashley thought. In about ten minutes she would be meeting Ross at the Student U. And this time she was going to turn him into Romantic Ross no matter what it took!

Ashley walked over to her dresser. She picked up her bottle of Dazzling Daisy and gently sprayed her wrists. "Oh, yeah, and I snipped off a tiny lock of my hair," Ashley added.

"Your hair?" Phoebe cried. "Why?"

"Not that much," Ashley replied. "Lucretia and Phineas exchanged locks of hair. Maybe it will help Ross become more romantic."

"Well, good luck!" Phoebe called as Ashley headed for the door.

Ashley strolled over to the Student U. She spotted Ross as soon as she walked in. He was sitting in his favorite beanbag chair, reading a magazine.

Ashley shrugged off her jacket and walked over to him. "Hi, Ross!" she said.

Ross smiled as he put aside his magazine. He stood up and kissed Ashley on the cheek.

A kiss! Ashley thought excitedly. *A good sign!*

"Did you notice the full moon tonight?" she asked. "I thought maybe we could take a nice long walk outside."

"In the middle of winter?" Ross said. "It's freezing out there, Ashley."

Okay, good point, Ashley thought. "Umm, then how about if we listen to some music?" she suggested.

Ross looked confused. "We already are," he replied. He pointed to the CD player. "The Wingnuts' latest CD is on. Isn't this your favorite?"

"Well, yeah," Ashley said, "but I was thinking of something more, you know, *romantic*. Like a violin concerto."

"A violin concerto?" Ross laughed. "Good one, Ashley. For a second I thought you were serious!"

Ashley frowned as Ross plopped onto the bean-bag chair and went back to his magazine. Clearly, being subtle wasn't going to work. She had to resort to more drastic measures.

Ashley reached into her purse for the lock of her hair. It was tied with a tiny piece of white ribbon.

Ross is going to love this, Ashley thought. *How many girls would cut off their hair for their boyfriend?*

Ashley knelt behind Ross's chair and dropped the lock of hair into his lap.

"Ahhh!" Ross yelped, jumping up. "What is that thing, a centipede?"

Ashley watched in horror as Ross stomped his foot on her lock of hair.

"Stop it, Ross! Stop it!" Ashley cried. "That is not a bug. It's my hair!"

"Your hair?" Ross stared down at the floor. "Did it fall off your head?"

"No," Ashley explained. "I cut it off because I wanted you to have it."

Ross looked totally baffled. "You want me to have *that*?" he cried. "Why?"

"Because Phineas T. Harrington III used to send Lucretia Arsdale locks of his hair," Ashley explained.

"It was considered very romantic in the 1800s."

"It's not romantic, Ashley," Ross said. "It's weird." He dropped back into the chair and opened his magazine.

Okay, last try, Ashley thought, taking out the white lacy handkerchief. She knew Phineas would stop to pick up a handkerchief if a lady dropped it. But would Ross?

Ashley glanced at her boyfriend. He was busy reading an article about the latest heavy metal band, Gag Reflex.

Why bother? Ashley asked herself. *Ross will probably pick it up and blow his nose with it.* She shoved the handkerchief back in her pocket.

"Hey, Ashley," Ross said, looking up from his magazine. "Want to split a candy bar with me?" He gave her an adorable smile.

Ashley couldn't help smiling back. "Sure," she replied.

Ashley watched Ross bob his head to a Wingnuts song as he went to the candy machine. Maybe she just had to accept that he wasn't the romantic type. But he was cute and nice and fun!

"Ashley," Phoebe exclaimed, rushing over. "I just got here. How did it go?"

"Phoebe, Ross will never be Phineas T.

Harrington III," Ashley replied. "And he won't be romantic like Jordan. But that's okay." She thought for a minute. "It's just . . . "

"What?" Phoebe asked.

"Well . . . Ross is great. But Jordan is so romantic!" Ashley said. "And the funny part is, Mary-Kate is so *not* romantic. She likes the Chicago Cubs and microwave pizza muffins."

"So?" Phoebe asked.

"So I know that Mary-Kate deserves a primo-supremo boyfriend," Ashley explained. "It's just that I wish those romantic letters were meant for me!"

CHAPTER TEN

"You guys," Mary-Kate protested as Ashley and her friends dragged her across campus toward the tree of love Thursday afternoon. "Do we have to do this now?"

"Today might be the day your secret admirer asks you on a date!" Cheryl declared.

"Big deal," Mary-Kate muttered.

"I think I see a letter," Phoebe said as they neared the tree.

"Go for it, Mary-Kate!" Elise exclaimed.

The girls gently pushed Mary-Kate toward the tree. She reached in and found a piece of paper.

"What are you waiting for?" Summer asked. "Read it!"

Mary-Kate rolled her eyes. Clearly her friends were way more excited about this love letter than she was!

"'My love,'" Mary-Kate read out loud. "'Meet me at the Founders Day Ball at eight on Friday. I will be waiting for you at the punch bowl.'"

Everyone cheered.

"You're finally going to meet your secret admirer!" Ashley said.

"Great," Mary-Kate replied. She wished she could feel as excited as her friends were. But she wasn't.

"Don't you want to do cartwheels, Mary-Kate?" Summer asked. "You must be so psyched!"

Mary-Kate folded the letter and shrugged. "After reading his letters, I'm not sure we have anything in common."

"What do you mean?" Ashley asked. "Of course you do."

"The two of us seem so different," Mary-Kate explained. "Can I help it if I'd rather watch a baseball game than a sunset?"

"Right on!" Campbell said.

"I want to meet a guy who is funny, nice, and into sports," Mary-Kate said. "You know. Someone like Jordan."

"Whatever happened with you and Jordan?" Elise asked.

"Nothing," Mary-Kate admitted. "I tried flirting with him, but I messed it up every time. Now he hardly talks to me. We didn't even hang out at the fencing demonstration this morning."

"Forget about him," Cheryl said. "Your secret admirer sounds awesome."

"And he sounds like he has amazing manners and perfect style!" Elise pointed out.

"So?" Mary-Kate asked.

"So if you're going to meet him, you'd better make sure you have good manners, too," Elise replied. "You have to come to my Victorian manners workshop."

"No thanks," Mary-Kate said. "I learned how to use a napkin years ago."

"Good manners in the 1800s included more than using a napkin," Elise informed her.

Mary-Kate shrugged. A manners workshop might be fun. "Okay, I'm there," she agreed. "When does it start?"

"In five minutes at the library," Elise said. She narrowed her eyes as she stared at Mary-Kate's sleeve. "But no way are you going with that mustard stain!"

"What mustard stain?" Mary-Kate glanced down at a yellow smudge on the sleeve of her jacket. "Oh, that. Someone bumped into me at the last Harrington football game. He was holding a hot dog."

"A proper Victorian lady would never wear a stained jacket to a manners workshop." Elise crossed her arms.

"But it's too late to run back to the dorm to change," Mary-Kate protested.

"I'll switch with you," Ashley offered. She handed her parka to her sister.

"Thanks," Mary-Kate said. She took the parka and gave her jacket to Ashley. Then she headed toward the library with Elise.

"Are there guys at this thing, too?" Mary-Kate asked as they entered the library's lecture room.

"Sure!" Elise said. "And a teacher or two. You grab a table while I get ready for my demonstration."

Mary-Kate looked around the room. Two lines of chairs were set up face-to-face around tiny tea tables. A bunch of First Formers were filing into the room and taking seats.

Mary-Kate slid into an empty chair. Then she noticed who was sitting across from her and gasped.

"Jordan!" Mary-Kate blurted out.

Jordan gave her a small smile. "Hi, Mary-Kate," he said. "What are you doing here?"

"Oh, you know, I always wondered which spoon to use with my oatmeal," Mary-Kate joked.

Jordan cracked up. "Yeah, me, too," he replied.

Mary-Kate relaxed a little. Things were starting to seem like old times between them!

"Good afternoon, ladies and gentlemen," Elise announced as she took her place at the front of the room.

"I guess that means us," Jordan whispered.

"First I will show you the art of sipping tea from a china cup," Elise went on.

Other students dressed as Victorian maids and butlers poured tea into the cups. When everyone's cup was full, Elise lifted a teacup for everyone to see.

"The proper way of holding a teacup is with the index finger and the thumb," Elise instructed. "And always remember to keep your pinky up!"

Mary-Kate and the others giggled as they carefully sipped from their cups.

"Any questions?" Elise asked.

"Yeah!" Jordan called out. "What do you do if your finger gets stuck in the cup handle?"

Everyone laughed as Jordan waved around a cup on his thumb.

"Always remember," Elise continued, "a well-mannered Victorian lady or gentleman always wipes her or his mouth after the first sip."

Some kids pretended to wipe their mouths with their sleeves.

"Very funny, you guys!" Elise complained. She cleared her throat and went on. "Victorians lightly dabbed the corners of their mouths with a napkin."

"What did they do when they ate barbecue?" Jordan whispered to Mary-Kate.

Mary-Kate giggled as she daintily tapped her lips with her napkin. She and Jordan were having the best time. So much that when the manners class was over, they decided to team up again. . . .

"Welcome to Victorian dance!" Cheryl announced inside the dance studio.

Mary-Kate stood next to Jordan while Cheryl and some other students demonstrated the waltz.

"Remember, gentlemen," Cheryl said. "Always keep one hand on your partner's waist. And, ladies, your left hand goes on your partner's shoulder."

The music began and couples started twirling around the room. Mary-Kate and Jordan laughed as they stepped on each other's toes.

"We are the worst dancers here," Jordan said.

"I know," Mary-Kate replied. "We should go to the ball together."

Mary-Kate froze. *Ohmigosh!* she thought. *Did I just ask him out?*

"I . . . er," Jordan stammered as his face turned red. "I already have a date."

Mary-Kate's heart sank when she remembered her secret admirer. "So do I," she said.

When the workshop was over, Mary-Kate and Jordan left the dance studio together.

"Sorry I stepped on your toes," Jordan said.

"That's okay." Mary-Kate smiled. "I think I stepped on yours more anyway!"

"Well, see you later," Jordan said.

Mary-Kate waved as he walked away. *I really wish I could go to the ball with Jordan*, she thought. *Why do I have to go with some boy I don't even know? And probably won't even like?*

The cold winter air made Mary-Kate sniffle. She reached into the pocket of Ashley's jacket for a pack of tissues. She found a bunch of blue papers instead.

What is this? Mary-Kate wondered. She read the handwriting on one of the papers.

"'Roses are red, violets are blue, I'm sick of oatmeal, how about you?'"

Mary-Kate's eyes widened. *These are my letters!* she realized. *But what are they doing in Ashley's pocket?*

Mary-Kate stuffed the papers back in the parka and started running toward Porter House.

Ashley better be in her room, Mary-Kate fumed, *because she has some explaining to do!*

CHAPTER ELEVEN

"I'm glad we ditched the dance workshop for the Victorian fashion show," Ashley told Phoebe.

"Me, too," Phoebe agreed. "With our passion for fashion, it was a no-brainer."

Ashley glanced around the half-filled auditorium. The stage was set up with a short runway sticking out into the aisle. There were no models on the runway yet—just an empty podium.

"I wonder if Mary-Kate is coming," Ashley said.

"Speaking of Mary-Kate," Phoebe put in, "when are you going to tell her that you've been helping with the letters?"

"Soon, I guess," Ashley replied. "But don't you think it's more fun for her this way?"

"No. It's more fun for you," Phoebe said.

Ashley slumped in her chair. *Phoebe's right*, she thought. *I was so excited about the secret love letters that I wasn't thinking about Mary-Kate.*

"Okay," Ashley agreed. "I'm going to tell Mary-Kate the truth the next time I see her."

"Good," Phoebe replied.

The audience applauded as Summer walked behind the podium. She was dressed in a long black skirt and a high-collared ruffled blouse.

"Is this thing on?" Summer asked, tapping the microphone.

Everyone covered their ears as feedback screeched through the auditorium.

"Oops, sorry." Summer glanced at an index card in her hand and cleared her throat. "Welcome to the Founders Day fashion show. All the clothes that you will see today are modeled after actual nineteenth century dresses that were worn by real women. They are available to wear to the Founders Day Ball."

Cool, Ashley thought.

"So let's give it up for—I mean—let's welcome our first model," Summer said.

A red-haired girl walked past Summer and onto the runway. She wore a deep purple hoop skirt with a black tasseled jacket.

"April is wearing a dress that belonged to Miss Hortense Weidemeyer," Summer explained. "She wore it for teas, socials, and to keep her dogs dry in the rain."

"Very cutting edge." Ashley giggled.

More models strutted out wearing Victorian skirts, blouses, and dresses. One even wore an outfit with puffy pants called pantaloons!

"And now for our final outfit," Summer said. "Here is Samantha, modeling a dress owned by Miss Lucretia Arsdale!"

"Lucretia Arsdale?" Ashley gasped.

"*Our* Lucretia Arsdale?" Phoebe asked.

A dark-haired model swept down the runway. She was wearing a tight laced-up bodice and the biggest hoopskirt Ashley had ever seen!

The skirt was dark green and embroidered with gold flowers and leaves. It was the same shimmering gold as the fitted top.

"Look at that lace! Look at that trim!" Phoebe swooned. "I want to borrow that dress for the ball."

"No way—it's mine!" Ashley exclaimed.

The model turned and the skirt swooshed out around her. Everyone applauded as the model walked back up the runway and off the stage.

"Lucretia's dress is not recommended for the

ball," Summer added. "Something about it being too wide for doorways."

"Forget it," Phoebe said. "I don't need a dress that comes with a warning."

"Well, I don't care," Ashley whispered to Phoebe. "I have to have that dress!"

"Thanks, everyone, for coming," Summer said. "Remember—all these dresses will be in the costume department after the show."

"Let's go get our dresses right now!" Ashley exclaimed.

"Okay," Phoebe replied. "But don't forget that you have to talk to Mary-Kate."

"I know, I know," Ashley said as the girls left the auditorium. "I hope she won't be too mad at me for replacing her letters."

"What did you do with them, anyway?" Phoebe asked.

"I kept them in my parka pocket," Ashley answered.

Phoebe stopped walking. "You mean the parka that Mary-Kate borrowed?" she asked.

Ashley froze. She had forgotten about lending Mary-Kate her parka. And she had forgotten about the letters!

"Oh, no," Ashley said. "What if Mary-Kate went

through my pockets and found all her letters?"

"Don't panic," Phoebe replied. "Why would Mary-Kate go through your pockets? The parka is probably hanging back in your room right now."

"I have to make sure," Ashley cried. "You go get our dresses. I'm going back to our room."

"Okay." Phoebe nodded.

Ashley ran all the way to Porter House. She raced up the stairs and flung open the door to her room. But when she stumbled inside—

"Mary-Kate! What are you doing here?" Ashley asked.

But the answer was obvious. Mary-Kate was sitting on Ashley's bed. And her letters were in her lap!

I'm in big trouble now! Ashley thought.

"Ashley, what are *you* doing with my love letters?" Mary-Kate shouted.

"Trying to help?" Ashley replied with a weak smile.

Mary-Kate held up the papers. "And if these are my letters, then what did my secret admirer get?"

Ashley's mouth felt as dry as dust. "Ummmm," she said slowly. "My . . . own . . . love letters?"

Mary-Kate jumped off the bed. "No wonder I had nothing in common with this guy," she cried.

"He wasn't even writing to me. He was writing to you!"

"But I did it for you, Mary-Kate!" Ashley said. "I wanted you to have the best chance you could with this guy."

"And you didn't think I could pull it off myself?" Mary-Kate exclaimed. "Thanks for the vote of confidence, Ashley."

Ashley felt terrible. *How can I make her understand?*

"Well, I really wanted you and this guy to get together," Ashley said quietly. "Especially since it's, um, Jordan."

Mary-Kate gasped. "Jordan?" she repeated. "The Jordan I like?"

Ashley nodded.

"Wait a minute," Mary-Kate said. "How do you know he's my secret admirer?"

Ashley took a deep breath. Then she spilled the whole story.

Mary-Kate sank onto the bed. "I can't believe you did this to me."

"I was only trying to help," Ashley repeated. "I knew you got nervous when you were around Jordan, so I thought maybe you could get together through letters."

Mary-Kate shook her head. "The weirdest part is that the Jordan I know is nothing like the Jordan in these letters!"

"Really?" Ashley asked.

"The Jordan I like is total goofball," Mary-Kate explained. "He's almost always joking around!"

Ashley wrinkled her nose. She usually didn't like guys who acted goofy.

"And Jordan is really into fencing," Mary-Kate added. "He's a total sports nut. Just like me!"

"Sports?" Ashley repeated. She wasn't into sports at all. Except maybe Ping-Pong.

"And," Mary-Kate continued, "Jordan once told me that when he runs out of clean sweat socks, he just turns the dirty ones inside out!"

"Inside out?" Ashley was horrified. That was worse than finger-licking and burping put together! From Mary-Kate's description, Jordan didn't seem romantic at all!

"That's why I can't figure out why Jordan would write stuff like that," Mary-Kate finished.

"Me neither," Ashley replied. "But I am really sorry about switching your letters."

Mary-Kate narrowed her eyes at Ashley. "I know," she replied. "But what you did still really stinks."

"I'm going to make it up to you, Mary-Kate," Ashley promised.

"How?" Mary-Kate asked.

Good question, Ashley thought. Then she remembered her beautiful dress for the ball. Whoever wore that dress would be the talk of the night!

"Mary-Kate," Ashley said, "I am going to help you knock Jordan Marshall off his feet."

"Forget it!" Mary-Kate cried. "No batting eyelashes. No twirling hair. And no *flirting*!"

Ashley smiled at her sister. "Who said anything about flirting?" she asked. "Just leave everything to me!"

CHAPTER TWELVE

"Can you believe women used to dress like this?" Mary-Kate cried.

It was Friday night and it was almost time for the Founders Day Ball. Campbell and Mary-Kate were in their room, getting dressed in their Victorian costumes.

Mary-Kate wore a long yellow-and-black-plaid dress with a black velvet vest. Campbell's sweeping purple dress was covered with ruffles.

"How do I look?" Campbell asked, twirling around.

"Like an overripe grape!" Mary-Kate joked.

Campbell laughed. "Just think," she said. "Girls couldn't play softball in dresses like this, or basketball, or even ride a bike. What did they do all day?"

"Faint!" Mary-Kate answered. "Dresses were laced so tightly in those days that I don't know how girls were able to breathe!"

"Well, their hairstyles were definitely cool," Campbell said. She grabbed her comb from the dresser.

Campbell and Mary-Kate shared the dresser mirror as they fixed their hair Victorian style. Campbell stuck a tortoiseshell comb in her short brown hair. Mary-Kate twisted her hair in two coils around her ears.

"Are you excited about meeting Jordan at the ball, Mary-Kate?" Campbell asked.

"Nervous is more like it," Mary-Kate admitted. "As soon as I tell Jordan the truth about my letters, he'll think I'm a pathetic poser."

"No, he won't," Campbell replied. "Those bogus letters weren't your fault. They were Ashley's."

The door swung wide open.

"Did I hear my name?" Ashley's voice sang out.

Mary-Kate turned toward the door. She didn't see Ashley—just billows of dark green material oozing through the door frame!

"Surprise!" Ashley said, peeking around the material. She gave the dress a big shove and stumbled inside the room. "Special delivery for Mary-Kate Burke!"

"What is *that*?" Mary-Kate gasped.

Ashley carefully laid the dark green dress and hoopskirt across Mary-Kate's bed. Then she patted down her own lavender-colored skirt and matching jacket. The outfit was trimmed with jet-black beading and black lace around the cuffs.

"It's your dress for the ball tonight," Ashley explained. "I borrowed it for myself but I want you to have it. Check out the size of the hoopskirt!"

Campbell whistled through her teeth. "This outfit is extreme," she said.

"A big dress makes a big statement," Ashley went on. "And this one has a very romantic history!"

"Romantic?" Mary-Kate repeated.

"It's my way of making up for the love letters," Ashley admitted.

This is really sweet of Ashley, Mary-Kate thought. "Thanks." She smiled.

"Well?" Ashley asked Mary-Kate. "Do you want to knock Jordan off his feet or not?"

Mary-Kate stared at the dress. The gold stitching against the dark green satin was really pretty. Definitely prettier than the dress she had on.

"You bet!" Mary-Kate said. She began taking off

her plaid dress. "Can you guys help me with that hoop?"

"Can't!" Campbell said. Her skirt bounced as she made her way to the door. "I have to set up the watercress and cucumber sandwiches on the snack table."

"Yuck," Ashley replied.

"Hey, they didn't have chips and dip in the 1800s," Campbell explained.

As Campbell squeezed out of the room, Mary-Kate wiggled inside the enormous hoopskirt. "I didn't think they made hoops this big!" she exclaimed as Ashley tied the skirt at Mary-Kate's waist.

Then Mary-Kate slipped the dress over her head. Piles of soft fabric fell into place around her.

"This dress is so gorgeous!" Ashley exclaimed as she laced up the bodice of the dress.

"How do I look?" Mary-Kate asked.

Ashley took a few steps back. She looked at Mary-Kate and clasped her hands.

"Like Lucretia Arsdale on her way to meet Phineas T. Harrington!" Ashley declared. "Now, hurry up. You have to meet Jordan at the punch table in ten minutes!"

Mary-Kate glanced in the mirror. *Not bad*, she

thought, looking at her reflection. She was definitely ready to meet Jordan face-to-face!

"Wish me luck," Mary-Kate said. Her heart fluttered as she made her way to the door.

Mary-Kate tried to step outside. But her hoop kept banging into the door frame.

"Ashley!" Mary-Kate cried. "I can't get through the door. The skirt is too big."

"I guess Summer wasn't kidding about the doorways," Ashley muttered.

Mary-Kate turned to face Ashley. "What do you mean?" she demanded.

"Nothing, nothing. It's no problem!" Ashley declared. "Just take off the hoopskirt and put it back on in the hall."

"I have to take the dress off first," Mary-Kate replied. She tugged at the laces of her bodice, but they wouldn't come loose. "Oh, no! The laces are stuck! Get me a pair of scissors, Ashley. I'm cutting my way out."

"I don't think so!" Ashley shouted. "You can't cut this dress. It's too gorgeous!"

Mary-Kate glanced at the clock and panicked. It was already five minutes to eight!

"Ashley, you have to get me out of here," Mary-Kate insisted.

"How?" Ashley cried.

"I don't know, but if I don't get to the ball on time, Jordan will think I stood him up," Mary-Kate said.

Ashley frowned. "I'm so sorry!" she said. "If I could trade places with you, I would!"

That's it! Mary-Kate thought. "You go to the ball and meet Jordan for me."

"Me?" Ashley squeaked.

"Yes, you," Mary-Kate said. "Pretend that you're me and knock him off his feet."

"But we haven't pretended to be each other in years," Ashley protested. "What if Jordan knows it's me? What if Ross sees me flirting with another guy?"

"Listen, Ashley," Mary-Kate said. "You got me into this mess. Now you get me *out*!"

CHAPTER THIRTEEN

How am I going to pull this off? Ashley wondered as she entered the Student Union. *Jordan will definitely know I'm not Mary-Kate!*

While Ashley hung up her shawl, she saw Cheryl handing out small white cards to the girls. The cards were attached to red ribbons.

Ashley took a card and slipped it around her wrist. Then she headed for the food table.

It's hard to tell who is whom, Ashley thought, looking around at the elaborate Victorian costumes. Most of the guys wore fake beards and hats. The girls wore fancy long dresses and elbow-length gloves.

The Student Union looked totally different, too.

Silver candleholders and old-fashioned portraits lined the tables and walls. A violin quartet in one corner played soft music as students waltzed across the dance floor.

Two girls brushed past Ashley. They were giggling and talking to each other behind huge Victorian fans.

That's it! Ashley realized. *I'll get a fan and cover my face!*

The orchestra struck up a fast song. Ashley watched as the girls placed their fans on a snack table and headed toward the dance floor.

I'm sure they won't mind if I borrow this, Ashley thought, grabbing a fan. She made her way toward the punch table.

A bunch of kids were clustered around a platter of dainty sandwiches. One boy wore a tall hat and a bushy beard.

Ashley looked closer. The brim of the boy's hat practically covered his eyes. He looked at an antique pocket watch and glanced around nervously.

That has to be Jordan, Ashley thought. She took a deep breath. Then she pressed the fan against her face and strolled over.

"Good evening!" Ashley said through the fan. "You must be my secret admirer."

"And you must be mine!" the boy replied.

"Well, it's not a secret anymore," Ashley said. "I'm Mary-Kate Burke!"

"Mary-Kate?" the boy repeated. "I'm Jordan Marshall!"

Ashley didn't know what to say next. What would Mary-Kate want her to say? Definitely nothing flirty!

"Did you enjoy my letters?" Ashley asked.

Jordan's beard wiggled as he grinned. "Your words were like jewels in a treasure chest!"

As Jordan chomped into a cucumber sandwich, Ashley began quoting one of her own love letters: "'My love is like a red, red rose that's newly sprung in June . . . '"

Ashley stopped reciting. Jordan was sloppily licking his fingers. Since when did a gentleman do that?

Ashley shook her head and went on. "'My love is like a melody, that's sweetly played in tune . . . '"

Now Jordan was sucking crumbs out of his teeth!

Forget you ever saw that, Ashley thought, fanning her face. *Just keep reciting.* "'He . . . loves me,'" she squeaked. "'He loves me—'"

"Bu-urp!"

Ashley stared at Jordan. What was going on

here? Finger-licking . . . teeth-sucking . . . burping . . . ?

"Ross?" Ashley asked. "Is that you?"

Ross sputtered sandwich crumbs in Ashley's direction. "How did you know, Mary-Kate?"

Ashley dropped her fan. "Because I'm not Mary-Kate. I'm Ashley!" she declared.

"Ashley!" Ross gasped. "It *is* you!"

"Why were you pretending to be Jordan?" Ashley asked.

"Why were you pretending to be Mary-Kate?" Ross replied.

Ashley smiled. "Okay, I'll go first," she said. "Mary-Kate wanted to meet Jordan, but she had a little, um, fashion emergency. So she asked me to come instead."

Ross took off his hat. "Well, Jordan was too shy to meet his secret admirer," he explained, "so he asked me to do it for him."

"That's funny," Ashley replied. "Jordan doesn't seem shy in his letters."

"Want to know a secret?" Ross asked. "*I* wrote those love letters. Not Jordan."

"You did?" Ashley's mouth fell open. The last person she would expect to write romantic letters was Ross!

Ross nodded. "When Jordan got the first letter,

he was too shy to write back," he explained. "So I wrote the letter for him and put it in the tree."

Ashley still couldn't believe her ears. The Harrington School Romeo was never Jordan—it was her own boyfriend!

"So where is Jordan now?" Ashley asked.

Ross shrugged. "He's around here somewhere. Probably hiding."

Ashley giggled. Then she laughed harder and harder.

"What's so funny?" Ross asked.

"I wrote the letters for Mary-Kate," Ashley confessed. "I was even the one who started the letter writing in the first place!"

Ross frowned. "What for?" he asked in a hurt voice. "So you could meet another guy?"

"No, no." Ashley shook her head. "I wanted to fix up Mary-Kate!"

"You know," Ross said, "I should have realized those letters were from you."

"Why?" Ashley asked.

"Because of your perfume!" Ross replied. "No one wears Dazzling Daisy the way you do."

Ashley blushed. Underneath all that finger-licking, teeth-sucking, and burping, Ross really *was* as romantic as Phineas T. Harrington III!

"So now that we've cleared that up, may I have this dance?" Ross asked.

"Of course," Ashley said. She held up her wrist. "You can be the first one to sign my dance card."

Ross took a pen from the table. Then he scribbled his name on all of the lines!

Am I lucky, or what? Ashley wondered. But before she could dance the night away, she had to take care of something else.

"We can't dance yet," Ashley said.

"Why not?" Ross asked.

"Because first I have to find Jordan," Ashley said. "And tell him the truth about Mary-Kate!"

CHAPTER FOURTEEN

Maybe if I eat enough chips, my dress will pop! Mary-Kate thought, grabbing a bag of potato chips from her desk.

It was a quarter past eight and Mary-Kate was still stuck in her room—and her dress!

She gave the knot on her bodice another tug, but it wouldn't budge. It reminded her of the knots she used to get in her ice skates back home in Chicago.

What did I do then? Mary-Kate wondered. She snapped her fingers.

"I know!" she cried. "I can use a safety pin to pick apart the knot!"

Mary-Kate shuffled over to the dresser in her big skirt. She found a saftey pin in a drawer.

Carefully Mary-Kate stuck the pin in and out of the tense knot. Until—

"Gotcha!" Mary-Kate cried as the knot began to untangle. She untied the strings of her bodice and shimmied out of the dress.

"Freedom!" Mary-Kate cheered. She glanced at the clock. If she hurried, she might still have a chance to talk to Jordan!

Mary-Kate put on the yellow-and-black dress and hurried out of Porter House.

When Mary-Kate reached the Student Union, she stopped outside the door. *What if Ashley is already pretending to be me?* she wondered. *I'd better check.*

Mary-Kate peeked in one of the windows. She saw Ashley running around the room, dragging a fuzzy-faced boy with her.

What is she doing? Mary-Kate thought.

Mary-Kate heard a twig snap. She turned her head and saw a boy peeking into another window just a few feet away.

Mary-Kate gasped. "Jordan?" she called.

"Huh?" Jordan asked. His eyes widened. "Mary-Kate?"

Mary-Kate stared through the window again. If Jordan was out here, then who was Ashley with in there?

"How come you're not inside?" Mary-Kate asked.

Jordan shrugged. "Umm . . . because I hate watercress sandwiches?" he said with a smile.

Mary-Kate giggled. Jordan looked really cute in his Victorian trousers, top hat, and coattails. Maybe she should try flirting with him one last time.

Or she could finally get real!

"Look, Jordan," Mary-Kate said. "I know you've been writing love letters and putting them in the oak tree."

Jordan's eyes widened. "How?" he asked.

"Because I wrote the other ones," Mary-Kate explained.

"You did?" Jordan gasped.

"Well, actually, Ashley wrote them," Mary-Kate confessed. "She didn't think my letters were romantic enough."

"I have a confession, too," Jordan said. "Ross wrote mine. I'm a total loser when it comes to writing corny stuff!"

Corny? Mary-Kate smiled. She *knew* Jordan wasn't that kind of guy. And she was glad!

"We should have just been ourselves all along," Mary-Kate admitted. "It would have saved us tons of trouble."

"Yeah," Jordan agreed. "But I'm glad my secret admirer turned out to be you."

Mary-Kate smiled shyly. "Then why did you keep running away from me?" she asked.

"I don't know," Jordan said. "I was just embarrassed, I guess. I'm kind of shy around girls I like."

Mary-Kate's heart did a triple flip. Jordan felt the same way about her as she did about him!

"So, do you think we can hang out sometime?" Jordan asked.

Mary-Kate wanted to jump up and down. "Sure!" she said.

Jordan took Mary-Kate's hand in his. Then they turned and walked into the Student Union together.

"That fruit punch looks pretty good," Jordan said. He grinned. "Would you care for a glass?"

"Spoken like a true Victorian gentleman." Mary-Kate giggled and bowed her head. "I would love some."

While Jordan went to the punch table, Mary-Kate eyed the couples on the dance floor. She couldn't wait to dance with Jordan!

"Mary-Kate!"

Mary-Kate whirled around. Ashley was running toward her.

"Is everything okay?" Ashley panted. "I've been

looking everywhere for Jordan! You'll never believe—"

"I heard the whole story," Mary-Kate cut in. "And guess what? After I told Jordan the truth, he asked me out!"

"That's awesome!" Ashley cried. "I should have let you be yourself from the beginning. I guess that's what boys really like."

"You bet!" Mary-Kate replied.

"So, are you ever going to try flirting again?" Ashley asked.

Mary-Kate smiled. "Sorry, Ashley. But not in a million years!"

PHINEAS T. HARRINGTON III:
Hopeless Romantic!
by Phoebe Cahill and
Ashley Burke

In honor of Harrington's 150th anniversary we would like to pay special tribute to its founder— Phineas T. Harrington III. As Mrs. Pritchard says, Phineas was one heck of a guy. But what is it that made him so special?

No, it wasn't because he had the largest silver coin collection in all of New Hampshire—or the longest beard. It's because Phineas is the most romantic dude in Harrington history!

Picture it: two estates, right next to each other. On one lived Harrington's founder, on the other, a beautiful woman named Lucretia Arsdale. The two met and fell madly in love. The problem? Lucretia's parents were making her marry some rich guy named Mortimer Baird (and boy was he ugly!).

Phineas wrote Lucretia love letters and left them in a white oak tree on her estate. Mortimer found out about the letters and challenged Phineas to a fencing duel. The winner would marry Lucretia.

Phineas was determined to win the hand of his one true love. But the night before the duel, Lucretia died. Phineas never got over his heartbreak. Years after he founded the Harrington School for Boys, he bought the estate Lucretia's family lived on and founded a second school in memory of Lucretia. Phineas named it White Oak Academy after the tree where he had left Lucretia's love letters.

Isn't that totally the most romantic story you've ever heard? BTW—that tree is still on campus if you feel like having a secret romance of your own!

GLAM GAB
by Ashley Burke

Fashion expert Ashley Burke

Girls, I will never complain about wearing itchy tights ever again. After what we learned from the Victorian fashion show I realized our generation has it really good compared to the women of the Victorian era!

Sure, those girls got to wear the most beautiful dresses in creation, but what went under those dresses was such a pain!

First, whoever invented the petticoat was insane. Women actually had to wear frilly, pleated, and huge pants under their dresses—even on a hot summer day! Can you say sweat-o-rama?

Then came the mighty hoopskirt. We all had experience with this one at the Founders Day ball. Okay, tell the truth ladies. How did you get yourselves into the bathroom stalls wearing this monster? The answer: You didn't!

And finally, the mother of all torture devices…the corset. You know what I'm talking about. The hard fabric that women tightened around their torso in the hopes of making their waist look smaller. All I have to say about that is: Owwwwww!

So the next time you're struggling to pull on those fitted jeans, just be thankful that fashion has come a long way, baby!

THE GET-REAL GIRL

Dear Get-Real Girl,

I really like this boy and I want to go out with him on Valentine's Day. So I decided to ask him! Here's the problem—he didn't respond at all! He just walked away. It was really weird. Do you think he didn't hear me or is that a sign he doesn't want to go?

Signed,
Soft-Spoken

Dear Soft-Spoken,

Hmmm. Just to be on the safe side, I would ask one more time. You could buy him a hearing aid and scream out your invitation just to make sure he hears you. But if you're not into

drastic measures, at least look into his eyes so you know he's listening. That way you're sure to get a response (no matter what that response may be)!

Signed,
Get-Real Girl

Dear Get-Real Girl,

I've been going out with this new boy, and I definitely like him. But every time he tries to kiss me— he burps instead! It is totally disgusting. I don't know why it happens. He never burps when we're just hanging out having fun! I know he's embarrassed, but I don't know what to say. Help!

Signed,
Belcher-Lover

Dear Belch,

You're right. That is totally disgusting. But I have a theory. Maybe he burps when he gets nervous! And I bet he's nervous when he tries to kiss you.

The trick is to catch him when he's not nervous. So here's the plan. The next time you guys are hanging out having fun, catch him off guard. Go in for the smooch! And let me know if it works!

Signed,
Get-Real Girl

ON GUARD!
by Mary-Kate Burke

Sports pro Mary-Kate Burke

Thank you, everyone, who came to cheer us on at the fencing demonstration last week. Not only does fencing look totally cool but it's a part of history, too! Here are some fencing facts you might not know:

1) It was one of the very first sports ever! It dates all the way back to ancient Egypt.

2) It is one of the six sports that has been played in every Olympic Game since the Olympics began.

3) In the Middle Ages, fencing was used to settle a score. There was no flipping a coin for these folks. They'd battle to the death!

4) If you're left-handed, fencing is the sport for you! It has been proven that left-handers have an advantage in technique and position. That's why

half of the world champions are lefties!

And girls, one more thing—fencers make the

most awesome boyfriends. Believe me, I know. Or at least, I hope to!

THE FIRST FORM BUZZ
by Dana Woletsky

Can it be true that someone is sending MKB love letters? Come on, 'fess up, MK. Who could possibly be *your* secret admirer?

Can someone explain why AB was seen throwing a

clump of hair at her boyfriend? She says it was romantic, but I say it's gross!

I heard that lots of interesting things happened at the Founders Day ball. The best was that PJ was so nervous dancing with EVH that he needed to hold three handkerchiefs under his hand to keep from sweating on her dress!

I didn't see much firsthand, though. My dance card was full within five min-

utes, so I didn't have time to snoop. It's hard being so popular all the time!

That's all, ladies and gentlemen. If you want the scoop, you just gotta snoop!

UPCOMING CALENDAR
Winter/Spring

So so so are you ready for the concert of the year? The new rock group, So So So, has been on their "What's Up, What's Up" tour for the past six months, and their next stop is our very own backyard! Call the box office in town for details.

What do Morons from Mars, Outer-Space Slugs, and Swamp Invaders all have in common? They're your favorite video games—and they're coming to a Student Union near you! Think you've got what it takes to break the high score? Show your skills on Friday night!

Have a crush on someone but you're too shy to tell him? Send him an anonymous rose through the Romantic Rose connection. And we promise that this year we won't tell who sent it—no matter how many chocolate candies he bribes us with!

Want to find out who is the most perfect couple on campus? White Oak's favorite couple's competi-

tion—the Dream Date Debate—is almost here! Sign up with your honey today.

IT'S ALL IN THE STARS
Winter Horoscopes

Aquarius
(January 20-February 18)

You're not usually one that goes out looking for attention—but this month the attention has found you! Instead of questioning why, just enjoy yourself! After all, Valentine's Day is approaching, and there's nothing wrong with having more than one Valentine!

Pisces
(February 19-March 20)

Pisces usually like to keep to themselves. But this month the stars urge you to get out there! If you don't feel like meeting new people, at least visit a new place or try a new class. There's a whole world out there for you to explore—don't miss it!

Aries
(March 21-April 20)

You know that boy you've had your eye on for the past few months? You're about to find out that he's not all he's cracked up to be! But don't worry, Aries. With your outgoing personality, you're sure to snag the guy of your dreams in no time!

#28: The Dream Date Debate

"Can you believe there's only one week left until the Dream Date Debate?" Mary-Kate said at morning announcements. She was sitting with her sister, Ashley, and their friends.

"I know," Ashley said. "I can't wait. Ross and I are definitely going to win!"

The Dream Date Debate was a tradition at White Oak. Couples paired up to answer questions about each other. Whoever answered the most questions correctly won the game—and a big prize!

"Quiet, everyone," Phoebe Cahill said. "Here comes The Head."

The headmistress, Mrs. Pritchard, walked onstage.

"Good morning, girls," she said. "I'm afraid I have some bad news."

May-Kate leaned forward. *What could have happened?* she wondered.

"Someone sneaked into Porter House last night after the lights-out and left a window open," Mrs. Pritchard said.

A few girls gasped.

Mary-Kate's heart pounded in her chest. She had sneaked out the night before to meet her boyfriend, Jordan! *But I'm sure I closed that window,* she thought.

"There were serious problems as a result," Mrs. Pritchard went on. "A raccoon got into Miss Viola's kitchen and scratched up the brand-new paint job on her kitchen cabinets."

I can't believe this! Mary-Kate thought. *Is this all my fault?*

"I expect the person responsible for this to come forward," Mrs. Pritchard went on. "Until then, the Dream Date Debate is canceled."

"No fair!" Phoebe cried.

"Whoever did it is going to be in major trouble," Wendy Linden said.

"Well, she had better confess," Ashley said. "She can't ruin the fun for everyone else."

Mary-Kate cringed. *If I confess, I'll be in big trouble. But if I don't confess, everyone will wind up hating me. What should I do?*

Win a **mary-kateandashley**

Spa Kit!

$100 value

Enter below to win everything you need to pamper yourself at your own private spa—all from the *mary-kateandashley* brand!

✴ *Hair care products*

✴ *Hairdryer and curling iron*

✴ *Lip gloss, body glitter, eye shadow and more*

✴ *Fabulous hair accessories*

TWO OF A KIND™
Spa Kit Sweepstakes

OFFICIAL RULES:

1. No purchase necessary.

2. To enter complete the official entry form or hand print your name, address, age, and phone number along with the words "TWO OF A KIND Spa Kit Sweepstakes" on a 3" x 5" card and mail to: TWO OF A KIND Spa Kit Sweepstakes, c/o HarperEntertainment, Attn: Children's Marketing Department, 10 East 53rd Street, New York, NY 10022. Entries must be received by July 31, 2003. Enter as often as you wish, but each entry must be mailed separately. One entry per envelope. Partially completed, illegible, or mechanically reproduced entries will not be accepted. Sponsors are not responsible for lost, late, mutilated, illegible, stolen, postage due, incomplete, or misdirected entries. All entries become the property of Dualstar Entertainment Group, LLC, and will not be returned.

3. Sweepstakes open to all legal residents of the United States, (excluding Colorado and Rhode Island), who are between the ages of five and fifteen on July 31, 2003, excluding employees and immediate family members of HarperCollins Publishers, Inc., ("HarperCollins"), Warner Bros.Television ("Warner"), Parachute Properties and Parachute Press, Inc., and their respective subsidiaries and affiliates, officers, directors, shareholders, employees, agents, attorneys, and other representatives (individually and collectively "Parachute"), Dualstar Entertainment Group, LLC, and its subsidiaries and affiliates, officers, directors, shareholders, employees, agents, attorneys, and other representatives (individually and collectively "Dualstar"), and their respective parent companies, affiliates, subsidiaries, advertising, promotion and fulfillment agencies, and the persons with whom each of the above are domiciled. Offer void where prohibited or restricted by law.

4. Odds of winning depend on the total number of entries received. Approximately 375,000 sweepstakes announcements published. All prizes will be awarded. Winners will be randomly drawn on or about August 15, 2003, by HarperCollins Publishers, whose decisions are final. Potential winners will be notified by mail and will be required to sign and return an affidavit of eligibility and release of liability within 14 days of notification. Prizes won by minors will be awarded to parent or legal guardian who must sign and return all required legal documents. By acceptance of their prize, winners consent to the use of their names, photographs, likeness, and personal information by HarperCollins, Parachute, Dualstar, and for publicity purposes without further compensation except where prohibited.

5. Five (5) **Grand Prize Winners** win a *mary-kateandashley* Spa Kit, which consists of $100.00 worth of *mary-kateandashley* brand beauty products to include: haircare products, hair appliances, cosmetics, and hair accessories. Approximate retail value of each prize is $100.00.

6. Only one prize will be awarded per individual, family, or household. Prizes are non-transferable and cannot be sold or redeemed for cash. No cash substitute is available. Any federal, state, or local taxes are the responsibility of the winner. Sponsor may substitute prize of equal or greater value, if necessary, due to availability.

7. Additional terms: By participating, entrants agree a) to the official rules and decisions of the judges, which will be final in all respects; and to waive any claim to ambiguity of the official rules and b) to release, discharge, and hold harmless HarperCollins, Warner, Parachute, Dualstar, and their affiliates, subsidiaries, and advertising and promotion agencies from and against any and all liability or damages associated with acceptance, use, or misuse of any prize received in this Sweepstakes.

8. Any dispute arising from this Sweepstakes will be determined according to the laws of the State of New York, without reference to its conflict of law principles, and the entrants consent to the personal jurisdiction of the State and Federal courts located in New York County and agree that such courts have exclusive jurisdiction over all such disputes.

9. To obtain the name of the winners, please send your request and a self-addressed stamped envelope (residents of Vermont may omit return postage) to TWO OF A KIND Spa Kit Sweepstakes Winners, c/o HarperEntertainment, 10 East 53rd Street, New York, NY 10022 by September 1, 2003. Sweepstakes Sponsor: HarperCollins Publishers, Inc.

Reading Checklist
andashley

ingle book!

It's What YOU Read.

- ❏ Calling All Boys
- ❏ Winner Take All
- ❏ P. S. Wish You Were Here
- ❏ The Cool Club
- ❏ War of the Wardrobes
- ❏ Bye-Bye Boyfriend
- ❏ It's Snow Problem
- ❏ Likes Me, Likes Me Not
- ❏ Shore Thing
- ❏ Two for the Road
- ❏ Surprise, Surprise!
- ❏ Sealed With A Kiss
- ❏ Now You See Him, Now You Don't
- ❏ April Fools' Rules!
- ❏ Island Girls
- ❏ Surf, Sand, and Secrets
- ❏ Closer Than Ever
- ❏ The Perfect Gift
- ❏ The Facts About Flirting
- ❏ The Dream Date Debate

so little time
- ❏ How to Train a Boy
- ❏ Instant Boyfriend
- ❏ Too Good To Be True
- ❏ Just Between Us
- ❏ Tell Me About It
- ❏ Secret Crush
- ❏ Girl Talk

Mary-Kate and Ashley Sweet 16
- ❏ Never Been Kissed
- ❏ Wishes and Dreams
- ❏ The Perfect Summer
- ❏ Getting There
- ❏ Starring You and Me
- ❏ My Best Friend's Boyfriend
- ❏ Playing Games

MARY-KATE AND ASHLEY in ACTION!
- ❏ Makeup Shake-up
- ❏ The Dream Team
- ❏ Fubble Bubble Trouble
- ❏ Operation Evaporation

Super Specials:
- ❏ My Mary-Kate & Ashley Diary
- ❏ Our Story
- ❏ Passport to Paris Scrapbook
- ❏ Be My Valentine

Available wherever books are sold, or call 1-800-331-3761 to order.

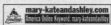

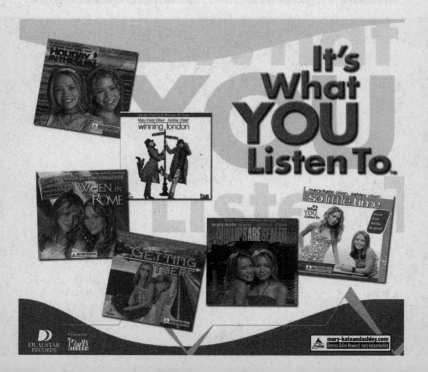